The Substitute

C. E. Shy

inner child press, ltd.

Credits

Author

C. E. Shy

Editor

hülya n. yılmaz, Ph.D.

Cover Design

William S. Peters Sr.
inner child press, ltd.

General Information

The Substitute
C. E. Shy

1st Edition: 2020

Publisher Information:
Inner Child Press International
www.innerchildpress.com

ISBN-13: 978-1-952081-25-5 (inner child press, ltd.)

$ 12.95

*D*edicated to my parents . . .

Clyde and Esterlee Shy

Table of Contents

The Substitute : Chapters

Table of Contents . . . *continued*

Acknowledgements

I thank The ALMIGHTY for the skills and all those who encouraged me to get published. My thanks also go to Russell Atkins, Everett Pruitt, Yaseen Assami, Diane Kendig, Bob Farmer, Bob McDonough, Norman Jordan, and my friend Nurrideen. Last but not least, I would like to thank my daughter Gloria Ware who kept reminding me of what I needed to do to complete this writing.

The Author's Disclaimer

The Substitute was published under the title of *Substitutions* by Uptown Media Joint Ventures on March 20, 2015 in its initial version.

This book has been written as nonfiction. Fictional aspects lie within the author's designation of names, characters, businesses, organizations, places and events. Any resemblance to actual persons – living or dead, events or locales is purely coincidental.

Preface

This is as much of my life as it's safe to remember, I think.

My life probably began not unlike the majority of the black people in the US. It wasn't until my last years in high school that I began to notice some of the many disparities that we were confronted with as African Americans. There were brothers and sisters who went through school getting good grades with expectations to land jobs and careers that would make life easier for them than what their parents had.

I had been writing since the seventh grade. When I look back over the years, I find what I wrote on was about separating myself from others. I was too young and unexposed to really understand how or when that would happen. In the meantime, I dealt with many things that kids did. Always being athletic, track and field, baseball and football were my pastime. That in itself limited my interaction with many other kids, and I found myself drawn to older girls and boys. At fifteen, I had girlfriends 18 and 19 years old. Most of them were in some way creative people.

I was never a good student and had poor grades throughout school to the chagrin of my parents. I think geography was my favorite subject. In fact, my interest for all the different places I wanted to travel to came from those courses. All along, I wrote. My first job was at an assembly plant. I encouraged the editor of the plant's newspaper to add a section called, "The Poets Corner". There was only one other person who contributed to the column, and she worked in the office. You have to figure that place was not a bastion of intellectual striving. I've looked through the archives of the company, trying to locate the poetry from the plant's paper. It may have helped to have remembered the name of the publication. It has been to no avail.

At that point in my life, I began to follow my mind's quest to travel. Before I started to plan on going to India, I was fortunate to meet a very good friend's brother. He was one of the Avant Garde music pioneers, Albert Ayler. He convinced me to go to Sweden for various reasons. He told me, the white people there were different than the ones here in the US. That was one of the many lessons I was to learn about stereotyping.

I purchased a one-way ticket to Stockholm, Sweden. I had no intention of ever coming back to the USA again. We plan, and God plans. He is the best of planners! I'm so thankful and grateful to my wonderful, tolerant parents for being there for me and my brothers. I could never repay them. If I had everything in this world to give them, it wouldn't be enough. After returning to the US, I was able to make comparisons between the country I left to the place I returned to. There was no comparison.

I remember being summoned to the draft board office. The person I talked to looked like a demon. All I could think of was how black people were being treated, no matter if they went to the military or not. They couldn't even vote on who their tormentor would be. As I sat there, I became outraged that she would talk that bull s… to me. The issue was resolved: We both agreed that I needed to stay a civilian. I later understood, she was just doing her job, she wasn't able to do it for me. I wasn't the status-quo brother. To this day, I remember that event. Eventually, I went back to Sweden. I knew a photographer who took pictures and sold them to magazines and other outlets. He lived in the same hotel I was in. I asked him to let me write something along with the photos. I would double as a model in different situations as well.

During my second time in Sweden, I picked up a bass violin at a place, called Nalen. It had very good natural acoustics. It was a place where musicians would gather after hours and jam till the break of dawn. Well-known professionals from all over the world would come there after their gigs were done that night. A funny thing . . . a band leader heard me fooling around on the bass violin and asked me if I wanted to play a gig in the north of Sweden. 'This is an obvious joke', I thought. It wasn't a joke. He explained to me why he said it. I was amazed. I still turned him down.

Upon my return to Stockholm, I was being hunted by Interpol for something that happened back in the

US. Joining me in Stockholm; though not being sought by any authorities, was Don Ayler, the younger brother of Albert Ayler. He began speaking with Al's old girlfriend, who at the time had a new boyfriend – a guitar player from the West Indies. After constantly bugging her, she told him that her uncle owned a hotel in a place called Jokkmokk which was located in Lapland, 20 to 30 miles above the Arctic Circle. He would be hiring there. She would call him and let him know he was on his way.

I was on the run anyway. So, off we went to see the uncle, hitchhiking after we ran out of money for transportation. It was in the dead of winter. We were on the E4 / European Route. We spent the nights in different places – heated barns, a dorm at Uppsala University, jail, etc. Some people allowed us to stay overnight in their homes. I remember one occasion when we sat at the dinner table, a small child was sitting next to me. He stared at me for a while, then took his finger to see if he could remove the color off my skin. It was hilarious! The north of Sweden was very remote and there are probably no black people to be seen. His parents were embarrassed. We weren't in the least bit offended. It was funny. I remember that we had to sign a guest book. I wonder at times about that kid and his family.

By the time we arrived in Jokkmokk, we were exhausted. The guy was indeed Al's old girlfriend's uncle and owned the hotel, but he was not hiring. He was nice enough to allow us to spend the night in very comfortable beds, and offered us a nice breakfast the next morning. Then he said he was sorry and wished us a safe journey. He gave us some money to get back to Stockholm. He may have felt some responsibility because of his niece.

Upon our arrival in Stockholm, Interpol was there to welcome me to jail and await my deportation to the USA. I was transferred to the local prison. Långholmen was the name. I happened to see some people I knew from the streets, well . . . sort of. I was going out with a gypsy woman whose grandfather left her a large house located not too far from a police station. She would harbor criminals on the run in the basement which was not in bad shape. I would meet some of them, get high and talk about different things. I spoke the language. She sold them weed and provided two meals a day at a huge cost. If and when they decided to move on or refused to pay more money, she would turn them in for a reward. So, when they saw me there in the same prison with them, they burst out laughing and said, "she turned you in too!"

There was a strange set-up at the prison. Right next to the men's section of the facility was the women's prison. The two buildings were connected, only separated by one door, as I remember.

Every day that you could go out on "promenade!" – what the guard called in a loud voice, the women would be at the windows showing themselves and screaming things at the men. The walking area was fenced off in 12 wedge-shaped sections with the guard tower being in the middle. Of course, you couldn't say anything to any of the women, just subtle gestures. Now that I think about it, they were pointing who they wanted to get it on with.

One day, the guy across the way from me called me over to his room. He asked me if I had seen the women next door. He said that, for a certain amount of money, he could fix it for me to have anyone of them. He was in jail for robbing a post office and getting away with several hundred thousand crowns. They never retrieved the money. He had a lot of influence in there. My question was how I could make money in prison. He said that he would talk to somebody and get me hooked up to fold envelopes and get paid.

When I saved enough money, I was able to have one of the women of my choice. I'm drawing a blank on the rest of the details. The cost of living didn't seem to be that much as I recall what I can recall. After months of fighting deportation, I was escorted back to the US by two detectives from the CPD. During the time I spent in Sweden, I wrote many poems and prose pieces.

While locked up, I was able to write a lot of things, especially with all the new experiences I gained. I ghost-wrote for two different writers and got paid. I made ends meet. I stayed in the county jail until my hearing. I was granted probation for three years. That's when I got really serious with the music. Sometimes I practiced all day long and traveled by bus to play at different places. At the time, my bass didn't have a cover. It must have been a strange sight. I started going to NYC to play with Albert and Don Sunny Murry and others in that genre. After the clubs closed, we would go to Leroi Jones' loft in the village. Everybody was there. The next thing I knew, the sun was up and it was time to figure out how we'd eat. I wasn't with that. I wasn't prepared to be a slave to the music and the puppet masters who would wait until you'd die, then get rich off of your efforts. When you are alive, they wouldn't give you a dime. The people who made those sacrifices deserve the credit.

The music that emotions garnered is still with me. I write it down. So, it's clearer most of the time when I say it. It can still be left up to interpretations. It wasn't much later that I decided to back down from playing for the reason I previously stated. I began to concentrate more on my writing. The times we were in were very turbulent, a period of time when young people were no longer buying into the status quo. It was a time for the various art forms to challenge the accepted norms. People were standing up against the things they felt was wrong within society. Whites as well as black people expressed a desire for change, civil rights movements and anti-war protests. In the opinion of many, the country was moving in the right direction. The writers' workshop I joined was headed by the Avant-Garde poet Russell Atkins. For me, it was a perfect match. The black nationalist movement constituted the hardliners of the struggle for civil rights. There was

Martin L. King and Malcomb X. Also, you had blacks that were involved with communist and socialist groups. I chose to be associated with the hardliners, and much of my poetry reflected those ideologies then and reflects them now.

Over the years, I have been able to be more or less, more or less. I had gotten married and had a son. So, a real job had to be considered. The movie *Uptight* was being filmed here in Cleveland at the time. I was one of the local militants chosen to partake of it. I can be seen in the opening of the Cleveland scene at a barbershop. We made some pretty good money. So, I quit my job and I was going to HOLLYWOOD! Well, . . . that didn't happen. In 1968, I was exposed to the religion of Islam once again. I guess this time was the charm.

After dropping the life I led along with the wife I had, I took my son and moved into a masjid, which was a huge, nearly empty building. I found a babysitter for my son. I didn't have any money. I worked for the babysitter, cutting grass, raking leaves and whatever she needed to be done. She was an older sister and was accustomed to raising other people's children. That phase didn't last long. I connected with a beautiful sister. She took charge of that son and we had two more sons. With my first Muslim wife, we had a beautiful son. Being still young and impetuous, at times, my life was changing faster than I could keep up with. These two sisters were and still are serving their families and communities. Before I went to Scandinavia in the early 60s, I had a daughter. It took a long time for us to finally get together. She is a jewel and the light in my life.

I stopped writing for three-and-a half decades. There was a major readjustment I had to make in order to continue. There was a lot to digest. A realignment of priorities. Cutting loose the ego. Coming to terms with who I am. I had to put first things first. I had to realize who was in charge. Once I did that, I was able to start all over again. While all that was going on, we established a prison program for Muslim inmates. Our primary goal was to keep them from returning to being locked up while attending to their spiritual needs. It was the first one of its kind in the country, recognized via contract as an African Muslim Organization. We had a very good working relationship with the wardens in all the institutions we worked at. There were people who didn't like the fact that we were accomplished. They went on to destroy it. The history is well-documented and can be found in the archives of the Western Reserve Historical Society and the George Mason University records and on a website called After Malcomb.

In 2015, I published my first book, *Time Share*. It is a novella. Then I wrote a short story collection, *Substitutions*. Unfortunately, the cost of registration was to run into a crooked deviant. I have been published 8 times in the county library system's poetry section, in four anthologies and as a consultant in two documentaries – one of which was co-dedicated to me. In total, I have 42 books published with 3 CDs, two compilation CDs and one single poetry CD. I am in the process of having my books republished through another publisher who has a sterling record with a wealth of experience to go with it.

If my head stays hot (and I don't have too much control over that), I plan to continue writing what I hear, see, feel, imagine, perceive and experience. INSHALLAH!

M. A. Shaheed
Proet / Verbalist

The Substitute

C. E. Shy

Chapter One

The Note

The Substitute

I find myself almost out of breath and blinded by what I remember of the mystery I saw in her eyes. I was fifteen years old at the time. She had to be close to that age. That was the first time I felt emotions I couldn't explain. The car seemed to move in slow motion as our eyes met. I became light-headed as she smiled at me. I remember thinking then that I would never see her again.

I was forty-two years old when I saw her again. It was her eyes that made me recognize her – they were unique. I remember them as if I had seen them ten minutes ago. 'I saw her first', I thought. I wanted to watch her before she noticed me. I wasn't sure that she would even recognize or remember me. She and two men were sitting at a table not far from where I sat. One was younger than the other. She was beaming. There was a glow about her and her eyes sparkled.

The waiter came to take my order. He was blocking my view of her.

"Sir, have you decided?"

"Yes, the wild Salmon."

"And what will you be having with that?"

I was caught up in the moment. "Sorry," I said. "Anything else, sir?" he asked again. "Green salad. No bread or starch. Olive oil and balsamic vinegar on the side."

"Thank you, sir."

I had been there four times since I arrived. This was the first time I saw her. The concierge at the hotel had recommended that restaurant. I always ordered the same thing. I guess, the waiter still had to ask. As he stepped away, I noticed that she was looking in my direction. Our eyes met again after two plus decades. She lowered her head and excused herself from the table. The two men she was with noticed the sudden change in her demeanor and began to look around the room. She looked up again and smiled slightly as she walked towards the back of the restaurant.

I was sure she remembered me now. If there was any doubt, it was gone. My mind began to race. *Is she married? Who are those men with her? What's her name?*

She was enigmatically beautiful. She was wearing a white dress that went down to the middle of her calf and tan sandals. Her arms were exposed. She looked 5'9" or 10" and about 130 pounds. Her hair was thick and came to the middle of her back. Her complexion was reddish brown. The dress she wore had to be tailor-made. It was amazing how it fit.

My mind took off again. *There is no way she could be unattached. No way!* If I could talk to her for just a few minutes, what could I possibly say? I was there on business. I couldn't afford to get distracted. It was too important for me to stay focused.

She wouldn't look in my direction for the duration of her time there, but you could see clearly, she wasn't the same as before she saw me. Her party got up to go. As she passed by my table, she smiled. I knew that the smile was for me. We connected. I had no idea what would happen next.

I was on an emotional roller coaster. I sat there with a straight face; inside though, I was hyped. She was gone again. I remember thinking, 'Could I have done or said something?' That was spilled milk now. I needed to let it go, and I did that well. In my prior job, a person's life depended on it. Eventually, I finished my dinner. It was late – about closing time. That had become my routine. I was usually one of the last customers to leave. I motioned to the waiter to bring the check.

On the tray with the check was a note written on a pink memo slip; it smelled of Jasmine. Before I could ask, the waiter explained, "I was asked to give this to you, sir. From the lady in the white dress. I'm sure you remember, sir." I laughed and said, "You are good!" He smiled and added, "I was asked to give this to you just when you were ready to leave." I gave him a hundred-dollar bill and told him to keep the change. He was very happy.

I opened the note. "Hello. My name is Velvet, and I do remember you. I hope to see you again soon. Tomorrow at 8:30 pm. Here okay?" My senses were being challenged. My thoughts were all over the place. I was emotionally shaken. The waiter asked if I was all right. "I think I'll be going now," I replied. As I left, I looked around the parking lot, hoping I might see her standing in the shadows, waiting for me to come out.

Why am I pursuing this? Where is this leading? All night long, these questions kept going through my head. I only had questions. No answers.

It was 2:00 a.m. and I still couldn't sleep. I had to be up first thing in the morning. A sleeping draught was the answer. It was 9:15 a.m. when I woke up. I did 300 crunches, 300 pushups and some stretching. I drank sixteen ounces of water. Then I took a cold shower. I was ready for my mission. The meeting was more important. I couldn't drop the ball on this. I felt I did enough to close this transaction. It meant a very large commission for me. I could take a vacation afterwards. I've been toiling away for a year – six days a week.

The meeting lasted five hours. Those damn lawyers were on the clock. When it ended, I was drained but I had closed the transaction successfully. When I got back to the hotel, my mind shifted gears. I took a power nap. I remember wanting to celebrate. I had almost forgotten about the night at the restaurant. I must have been out of my mind!

How did I manage to get my senses back together? After 350 crunches and 200 pushups, I took a shower – my second of the day. I listened to some Reiki healing music for about 20 minutes. I was back to where I left off the night before.

The Substitute

Chapter Two

A Night of Anticipation

The Substitute

It was 7:30 p.m. and it was 95 degrees outside. I wore a tan linen suit with short sleeves, a pair of brown sandals – no socks. I had put that outfit out before I left for the meeting in the morning. These were the clothes I was going to wear to "The Capital". When I exited the elevator to the lobby, a lady approached me. She was at the meeting that morning. She asked me to have a drink with her later if I had time. I politely accepted her invitation.

I arrived by taxi at the restaurant at 8:15 p.m. That was the first time I ever really paid attention to the name. I entered, glancing around the room, and was seated right away. I sat in the same seat as always. The rain started to pour down. You could hear it on the glass roof.

The temperature inside was comfortable at maybe 70 degrees. The place was full of customers who were conversing, drinking and seemed to be having a good time. "The Capital" had an excellent chef. I found out later that the restaurant was rated four stars. It's the chef that justifies the rating.

The same waiter was there and told me that the lady was powdering her nose. Then he asked me if I needed a menu. I laughed and said that I might try something new tonight. He smiled broadly and went to get one. This guy had a good sense of humor. He reminded me of a street guy I knew who turned his life around. He had good instincts and was perfect for the job. As he returned with the menu, Velvet was coming from the back of the restaurant. As she approached, she smiled, and I stood and extended my hand. Her hand felt like silk. It was hot; her fingers were like those of a concert pianist. It was as if we were the only ones there.

"My name is Amir."

She sat across from me. "That is an interesting name. What does it mean?"

"It is an Arabic name. It means commander."

"You mean as in the army?"

"More or less."

"Have you ever been in the army, Amir?"

"No, I've always been a peace activist."

To that, she smiled. "Me too."

I tried to hide my excitement, but she saw right through me. I was hooked! Most of the time she spoke, I tried to keep my eyes off her not to reveal myself too much. All kinds of emotions were coming together all at once.

She was wearing a loose-fitting cotton outfit. It was yellow. Her hair was pulled up, displaying the elegant features of her face. Her skin was smooth and radiant. While asking me if I was cold, she got up and sat next to me. The air was blowing directly on her. As she sat, she commented, "That's much better." I could feel the heat of her body on mine. I felt like I was paralyzed. She was dictating the pace. I was just trying to keep up. That wasn't good. I smiled at the thought. As brief as it was, she saw my reaction and asked me if I was okay.

"Sure, sure," I said.

Looking directly at my eyes, she asked: "So, Mr. Amir, who are you?" She crossed her leg and it was touching mine.

"I am a businessman who happens to be in your city on business, who also finds himself face to face with someone he has not seen in at least two decades, never has spoken with or been this close to before. And . . . I'm not at all disappointed."

"I always wondered what happened to you or if I would ever see you again. I'm not at all disappointed either."

We ate and talked. We laughed. Her body was pressing against mine, with no room between us. Time slipped away. I pointed out that it was getting late, that most of the customers had gone and the employees probably wanted to go home. She also thought that was most likely the case. But she then told me that she was the owner of the restaurant and that they would understand. Then suddenly she said, perhaps I was right, and that she hoped I wasn't sleepy, as the night was way too young. She added that I looked like someone who would appreciate Charlie Parker, Miles Davis, and John Coltrane. All I could do was laugh. Those were my favorites. "Let's go if you are ready."

"Yes, I'm ready to go."

The valet retrieved her Cayenne in a hurry. "Have a good evening, Ms. Velvet and you as well, sir." She signaled the valet to give me the keys. I took them and tipped him. I pushed the ignition button and asked, "Which way?"

"The GPS will give you the directions."

"How long have you lived in this city?" I asked.

"This is where I got married. My husband is from here."

"Your husband!" I exclaimed. "Is there anything else I need to know? Is he at home waiting with a pistol?"

"No," she responded with a laugh, "we've been separated for a year and I've filed for a divorce. In fact, I filed yesterday."

"Where is he now?" I asked, feeling a little uncomfortable.

"He lives in Niger and has an oil and gas drilling business. He hasn't been back to the US in over a year."

"Is this divorce by mutual consent?" I wanted to know.

"Not really. I wanted children but he couldn't have any. Plus, the fact that he was too far away . . . I didn't want to live in a jungle."

I had heard everything she told me, and somehow none of it mattered. All I knew was that I was with her now and I was happy about that. I was glad he was in wherever.

Velvet asked, "Are you married?"

"No."

"Do you have any children?"

"Yes, two boys."

"That's great. You are fortunate," she replied whimsically.

The GPS directed us to a stately house. It was gray and white with a lot of flowers around it. I couldn't make out the varieties; but I could smell them. When I turned into the driveway, a huge gate came into sight. It had to be at least ten feet high.

"One more question. No more after this. Do you still love your husband? He is still your husband! Just because you are getting a divorce doesn't mean you don't love him."

"At one time I did. I think we just grew apart," she answered. "As for us, I feel you and I can relate."

When we pulled close to the door, all the lights came on. It was like daytime around the whole house. "Hey, that's impressive! I like it!" I said.

Then I commented, "I just knew you had to be married when I saw you."

"Why?"

"Because women as beautiful as you are usually married, unless they are crazy or something else."

She told me that she didn't want to be alone that night and thanked me for being there. I told her that I felt privileged. We got out of the vehicle, and as we walked toward the house, the housekeeper met us at the door. Her name was Sarah. She had a blank dutiful expression on her face.

Once inside, we walked through a short hallway towards a wide staircase and ascended the stairs to the second level of the house. I started to see that this lady was very well-to-do. She wore a Rolex watch surrounded with diamonds, two diamond rings that had to be at least 4 carats each, and a chevron necklace.

The house was immaculate. There were Persian carpets – from Tabriz, Afghani and Chinese carpets everywhere. The housekeeper watched us until we entered a room upstairs. Velvet was wearing some kind of a flower scent. All these things working in concert led me to a point what I assumed then to be my destiny. It was like some spell that had been cast. I was all the way in.

I asked her about her perfume. She created it. "Let us call it 'Ours' tonight." I told her that I couldn't have thought of a better name. She told me that she owned a fragrance boutique downtown and that she had a degree in chemistry. Ever since she was a little girl, she wanted to create scents that people would enjoy; now fashioning fragrances to suit the personalities of her clients.

At that moment, I thought of what the waiter told me at the restaurant just before Velvet came to the table. He had spoken in a low voice, "No disrespect, sir, but the lady has been approached by many men of all kinds. She never even looked at them twice. We knew somebody would attract her attention. You got it, sir. Our hats are off to you!" I remember thinking how many times I had been in similar situations. The reasons were different and the outcomes were not good for the other parties.

As we proceeded up the stairs, a room situated off to the side came into view. When we walked through the door, the lights came on and a diffuser began to emit the scent of Jasmine. There was a smaller room inside. A love seat was positioned near an aquarium where about twenty fish in many different colors seemed to swim to the music. Miles Davis was playing – first, "It Never Entered My Mind," followed by "When I Fall in Love". I began to sing along, putting the lyrics in their places.

"Do you drink coffee?" she asked. "I do tonight." Not being a real coffee drinker, I took a sip and asked, "What kind of coffee is this?" "Jamaican Blue Mountain." I thought to myself, 'I drank so much coffee when I was with the agency that I never wanted to see another cup of coffee. We never had this kind though. This isn't bad at all!'

The Substitute

Chapter Three

The Morning After

The Substitute

We talked some more; we covered a lot of subjects. I asked her if this was a dream. She said that she hoped not because that meant she would be dreaming too. I told her; I wouldn't want this to be a dream unless it was to come true. I remember asking her how she would like this to end. Her response was, "Never."

Then we didn't speak for a while. We just listened to Parker play "April in Paris" and "Autumn in New York." Coltrane played "Welcome." I broke the silence by asking her if she lived there alone. The maid lived there and the groundskeeper lived in the house in the back. She had two pit bulls back there too. They were never allowed in the house but they were being pampered. "I also have a cat, and as you can see, many fish."

She changed the subject to us, telling me that she knew she would like me. I told her that she was a world apart from any woman I had ever met before. She asked me if I really had to go the next day. "Yes, but I could be back in five days. I have some vacation time coming. Three weeks." She openly showed her excitement, "That's great! I'll look forward to that. In that case, we have a date." "Yes." 'I could not have written this', I thought. All of this was also more than luck.

She left the room, then returned shortly, wearing a blue sculptured dress that came down to her ankles. Her hair was pulled back. The room's fragrance had been changing gradually. I was familiar with that scent. I used to go to a shop in New York City that sold that perfume; I had not experienced that in a long while. "Sandalwood?" She clapped her hands and said, "You have a good sense for scents." "Thank you, ma'am."

The time I spent with her is locked in my mind. I will never forget her. I felt weak for falling for her so fast and so hard. She sat down next to me. Her body was warm, soft, and she was wearing a scent I recognized immediately –

Heliotrope. I wanted to touch her. She got up from the sofa and offered me more coffee.

I asked her if she had any plans sleeping. "No! And neither do you." I did not know if that was meant to be ambiguous or that she was setting the agenda. I could hardly wait for her next move.

In another room, there was a bar, an old- fashioned jukebox, a larger sofa and a diffuser dispersing an array of fragrances. She told me that, when the door was closed, the room was soundproof. I couldn't keep my eyes off of her. I was not near being sleepy. Whatever was going to happen, I wanted be wide awake to see it or be in it.

Her body was sculpted. I couldn't possibly forget those dimensions. She was about 5'9" and 130 pounds. She was agile, clever, educated, witty, intelligent, beautiful and rich. This was the little girl whose eyes had met mine. It seemed a lifetime ago.

The night lingered on. She asked me what time my flight was. "12:35 a.m." "Is that tonight or tomorrow?" she asked. "I've lost track of time. What time is it anyway?" She responded playfully: "Nowhere near the time for you to leave. So, relax. If you really want to know, it's 3:36 a.m. Are you tired?" "Absolutely not!" I answered.

"I want to be with you every waking moment. You know Amir, you are the only man who has ever stepped in this room. I mean, of interest to me personally. My husband was in Africa when I purchased this house. He was supposed to be here when the transaction closed; but he told me that something came up and that he was not able to travel."

Then she asked me, "How old are you, Amir?"

"I'm 42."

"I turned 39 today."

"Are you kidding me?"

She told me that today was her birthday and I was her birthday gift. I asked where the cake is and that I needed to jump out of it! She held out her arms, saying, "I'm the cake. When you came into my restaurant that day, I remembered you. My dad and my brother wondered what was wrong with me. I was overcome with emotions. I had to gain my composure. That's when I wrote that note to you. I told Toby to give it to you when you were getting ready to leave. It feels right and good being with you, Amir." "Ditto!" "I want you in my life, Amir!" "I am here," I replied in a soft voice.

I began to sing in her ear "Blue Velvet," a song by a group whose name I couldn't remember. Then I played it on my phone. She closed her eyes and said nobody sings like that anymore. She started to cry. I dried her eyes with my handkerchief. She had never heard of that group. I told her that I grew up around aunts and uncles, and that's how I knew about old groups. I told her that I thought the song fit the occasion.

She changed the subject to tell me about something she had done on a whim. I asked, "What is it?" One day in a department store, she went to the men's section and purchased a pair of blue pajamas. The size was 2X. "There was no good reason for me to buy them. I don't know why. I just did it." "Everybody does something similar sometime," I reacted. She then asked me what size I wear. I laughed before I said, "3X." "These are yours now." I thanked her.

Now was the right time for me to lead. I pulled her close to me; she threw her arms around my neck and kissed me with no inhibitions. She tilted her head back, looked at me and then the ceiling, eyes half shut, then kissed me again. I don't know for how long. She ran her hand over my torso, and said, "Your body feels as hard as a rock." She took my hand and led me to her private chamber.

The alarm clock sounded like it was inside my head. I did not move. I told her I was afraid to wake up because she may not be there if I did. She bit me on the ear and whispered, "I'm here." It was 11:38 in the morning. She pulled the covers over our heads and kissed me gently on the lips. I was as far in love as a human could possibly get. The shower, made of polished concrete, was big. There were two shower heads; one of them was scented with lavender; the other, with citrus.

She demanded that I put the PJs back on. I did. She wore a light pink gown; no slippers. Brunch was on the table downstairs. While we ate, we talked about our ancestry, music, food, exercise and travel. Everything but the future – it just never came up. It seemed to be understood that the future was ours together. She asked me if I could check out of the hotel now. We could then go to the airport from her home. I agreed.

We left for the hotel. I gathered my belongings. I checked with the desk clerk for any messages. There was one. It was from the secretary at the office where the meeting took place the day before:

Thank you for coming. We all felt that the meeting was very productive. It was a pleasure to meet you. Hopefully, you will return to our fair city. It will be my pleasure to show you around.

Sincerely,

Mary Taylor
Cell Phone: 229-711-0090

I balled the note up and discarded it in a nearby ashtray. Velvet picked it up, read it, and said, "That's not going to happen." She tore it into small pieces, took it outside with us and threw it into the garbage bin. Then she dusted off her hands. As if to say, that's that. There was no conversation on the subject matter.

Chapter Four

A Day of Anticipation

The Substitute

We went back to her house. She took me on a tour of the property. There was a large garden with cherry and apple trees. Various vegetables were growing in another part of the garden. The dogs seemed to adore her. She petted them. Their area was spotless. They were well taken care of.

I met George, the ground keeper / security guard. He was an ex-NFL player. He still looked like he was ready to suit up for a game. She told me later that he was injured and had to quit playing. So, she hired him. There was a swimming pool and a first-class workout facility. If you couldn't get it done there you weren't serious. She took me by the hand and pulled me into the small green house, dug her nails into my back and kissed me violently.

We stayed there for a while. When we continued the tour, I noticed the monitors on the house and the motion sensors on the ground. There were 10-foot-high privacy fences around the entire property. The security was tight!

Top security or not, I was primarily thinking, 'How does a woman look more beautiful than she did the day before?' I had even concluded that it had to be my imagination, because it seemed like as if her beauty was ever-evolving. I told her that I felt like last night was my birthday. She said it was the birth of a relationship that she hoped would not end.

We were nearing the last moments of our first time together. We exchanged contact information and continued to stroll through the garden. George looked up now and then. When our eyes met, he gave me an approving nod. I turned to Velvet, "He seems to be a loyal guy." She said that they were lucky to have him.

"I wish I had met you before you married."

"I am grateful that we met when we did."

We walked to the gate in the back, then to the river's edge. We stood there for a while and watched our reflections dance on the water. I told her that I would text her when I arrived at my destination. "No, call me. I want to hear your voice. Then, I can sleep." "Okay."

Dinner was served. I asked her how often she cooked. She did so rarely. She then told me that she was a graduate of a highly prestigious culinary school in France, and occasionally, she would get the urge to prepare a meal. She knew that Sarah was more than adequate and capable, as she had graduated from the same culinary school. I was quite familiar with that school. In fact, I used to live only a few blocks from there in France.

I arrived home at 3:35 am. As soon as I walked in, I called her. I was feeling like a 15-year old again. She answered right away: "Hi, are you home?" "I just walked in the house." "I can sleep now. I miss you already." "Me too." "Good night, Amir." "Good night."

We didn't talk the next day. We were both busy people and had to focus on our daily activities. I remember thinking about what kind of a future we would have together. I wondered if we would even have one. All this seemed too good to be true. I guess, some of the best things happen when you don't make plans.

Chapter Five

Half on a Baby

The Substitute

I went into Jack's office. Jack was my boss. We knew each other from the agency. I never worked with him in that world. He hired me when I left the agency. It was an easy sell for me to get this job.

He got up. He was a big guy with the demeanor of a drill sergeant. He had a huge smile on his face. He stuck out a hand and spoke in his thunderous voice, "Congratulations, Amir! That deal is going to put us over the top in reference to our projection for this year."

"Thanks Jack. Oh, by the way, I wanted to let you know. I am going to take my vacation now."

"I certainly hope so. You didn't take any time off in a year! You need to do that."

"I'll start Friday."

"Sure. If you need anything, I'm here."

Jack still had a lot of our old life in him; I guess we all did. "Okay, Jack. Thank you." "No. Thank *you*, my friend!" We shook hands. I left.

When I got home, it was 5:30 pm. My computer was pinging. Velvet was making faces and sticking her tongue out. She had written in bold letters, "CALL ME!" I did so right away.

She started talking as soon as she picked up the phone: "I have some news. I don't know if it is good or bad; you will tell me, Amir."

"What is it Velvet?" I asked her with some apprehension.

"I missed my period. It is like clockwork – it never deviates. Just so you know, Amir, I want to be pregnant. I want to have this baby, your baby!"

After a brief moment of silence, I uttered, "If you are happy, then I'm twice as happy. Don't you think that it's too soon to assume so, though?" "No, I can feel in my heart that this is it."

"Wow!" I said, trying to get a grip on what was going on here. There were a ton of emotions running through me. Things were moving too fast!

"When are you coming back, Amir?"

"I'll be there Friday at 9 pm, God willing."

"If God is willing, I'll be there to pick you up. I've asked God not to leave me barren."

"Sweetheart, I don't want you to be disappointed. It could be a false alarm."

"No, Amir. I know it is real. I know it! I felt it when it happened." She spoke with so much conviction that I didn't say another word. She then added, "I have to go now. I've fallen behind in all my work. I'll talk to you later, okay?"

"Okay. Take of your business. I'm here." I was thinking, 'What is this? What the hell? Man, oh man! What's next? This is really moving fast!'

I remember not really being upset. I just didn't know where this was going. It wasn't difficult to imagine me being with her, raising a son or a daughter, though I never saw myself being in that situation again. Neither could I imagine being without her. Here I was, a top negotiator, ex-top agent, mixed up and off balance. Everything was happening so fast. I decided to turn my full attention on my job until Friday.

When I talked to Velvet on Thursday, she told me that she was clearing her desk to make sure there would be minimal interruptions when I arrived. We only talked sporadically during those few remaining days. I was going to stay with her. I thought of every possible scenario. The "whats", the "whys" and the "hows" were running through my mind. I was trained to ask those questions. All my life, I had to struggle hard to get the things I got. This seemed too easy but I liked it, and I was going to follow it through to see where it was going. I was hooked and she was running the program. I had never been happier. 'That sounds sick, but that's where I'm at right now,' I thought.

Chapter Six

Sweet Chemistry

The Substitute

It rained for two whole days and nights. We spent a lot of time reading, exercising, and in her green house. Sarah showed her culinary skills at meal times. There were fresh cut flowers at dinner every night. Velvet had special flowers there for her business. I watched her concentrate on her work. She was focused. I called her the Dr. Frankenstein of the perfume business. She was not going to be distracted.

She gave me some backdrop information on how she managed to secure contracts with major French perfume companies to develop new fragrances. I saw her catalogs. She had her own wealth – independent from her husband's. She was an amazing woman. Her beauty and her mind were in parity. At one point, she had considered leaving the business and just travel. She asked me if I had traveled much. I told her, "yes". She asked me where.

"I lived in the UAE, Egypt, London, Paris, Stockholm, Senegal, Trinidad, Jamaica, Guyana, Tunisia, and Paris. I visited many other places like Nigeria, Holland, Norway, Germany and South Africa."

"I'm envious."

"Maybe we could travel to some of these places together one day."

"God willing." She then asked, "What did you do for a living?"

"I worked for a public relations firm that offered countries insights into American art and culture. I was a musician, poet and writer. I learned as much as I taught."

She seemed to be trying to get some idea on who I was, what I did; all of which made sense, especially under those particular circumstances. She asked about my current job, what I did there, how long I worked there. I told her, I was under contract with an international mining firm's head office in NYC and that they had offices in Europe, Asia, the Middle East and Africa. I told her that this was like interviewing for a job. "In a way, you are." "Clever lady." I said and laughed.

"I want to know more about my baby's father."

"You keep saying that, sugar, but we have to wait and see." I had to remind her again. She was not listening to me. She asked me if I was excited. I told her, I try not to get too excited about anything because every time I do, I get disappointed.

"You know, Amir, I'm not getting any younger."

"I understand, baby. But I've learned over the years that patience is really a virtue."

She told me that during the very first minutes she spent with me that night she knew I was different and she wasn't going to let that get away from her. "I pray that I'm pregnant with a son from you. That night, I opened up to you completely. Before you leave, we'll know if it's true." Tears were welling in her eyes. I told her it would be very easy for me to be with her to the end.

We visited her shop on Main Street and Riverside. The shop was only a short distance from her house and the restaurant. Out front were Mercedeses, Bentleys, Porsches, and a host of similar high-end cars. We went through the rear entrance. I met the manager. She was stunning. She was perfect for the job. She gave me the once-over and then smiled at Velvet. There must have been fifteen or twenty women out there and three or four men. Some of the transactions totaled five hundred, fifteen hundred, and a thousand dollars; it was remarkable. I caught a glance of Velvet watching me for any reactions. I had none. That was elementary. I could see clearly, though, how she made some of her money.

Time seemed to be flying. I was nearing the end of my second week there. Everything had been nothing less than extraordinary. We were connected.

Chapter Seven

Hiding out in the Open

The Substitute

The next afternoon, she asked if I thought that it would possible for me to relocate to her city. She told me that she was well-connected, and she would help me set up an office. I told her that I didn't know but it would not hurt to inquire; it all depended on the direction of the company.

"You don't miss a thing, do you?"

"I try not to." Then she added, "I am going to dine with some friends tonight in their home. Would you mind joining me?"

"No, of course not."

"They are kind of an artsy type. I'm sure you will get along with them just fine as long as you don't recite the things you whispered in my ear." I smiled and said, "For your ears only."

"Mr. Barksdale considers himself a poet and so does his wife Hilda. They spend a lot of money for my business. They have a lot. This should be very interesting." She spoke gleefully. I told her that I thought I could remember a few of the ones I wrote. "I'm good. Real good." "Wow! EGO! I never saw that side of you before, but I could tell the first time I saw you walk that you are very confident. I also think you can be very violent if provoked."

"You see a lot of stuff that isn't there."

"RIGHT!" she replied.

We arrived at her friends' estate. I do mean estate! You could put Velvet's place inside theirs. It was on what appeared to be six acres of land. She told me it had 12 bedrooms, 10 bathrooms and four half baths. I asked if it was just the two of them there. "Yes, for the most part." That was just the tip of the iceberg. "They have two boys and two girls. Both are very well off in their own right. Then there are the many grand kids. The Barksdales do a lot of entertaining. They deal with the who's who of politics and the business world." I was impressed.

The Barksdale's maid greeted us. She escorted us to a room where Mr. and Mrs. Barksdale were waiting. Mrs.

Barksdale gave Velvet a big hug, then complimented on her outfit. Mr. Barksdale put his hand out, and I shook it. At first, I thought there was a contest of sorts with handshakes. I asked to use the bathroom, where I washed my hands thoroughly. I then joined the group. Right at that point, the maid announced that dinner was served. The meal was well-prepared, mostly vegetarian, with a small portion of scallops, I think. It seemed that all conversation was going to be reserved for after dinner. We retired to a well-lit sitting room. Velvet and I sat in a love seat. Our hosts sat in two chairs divided by what looked like a table and a lamp that was hand-carved from teakwood. The piece was unique.

I was introduced as a friend and a writer. Our hosts went along with that introduction but looked a little suspect as if that was really all there was to the relationship.

The couple had to be in their mid to late sixties. They looked like money. Velvet had met them for the first time when they came into her perfume shop, then again at her dining establishment.

He was a real estate developer all over the country. His wife was a real estate agent and made very large commissions.

"Well, young man, what brings you to our city?"

"I like the scenery," I answered, cutting my eyes at Velvet.

His wife said, "I understand you are a writer."

"Well, not full time, but I do write. I've been published a few times."

Mr. Barksdale asked me when I started writing. "In seventh grade," I replied.

Velvet watched me interact with them. She didn't say much. I wondered if this was an audition.

The night went on. It was actually a good night. I didn't think I could remember as many poems as I recited. Whenever I recited anything too romantic, Velvet tapped me on the leg. The Barksdales read several they had written. Hilda commented, "Velvet, you haven't said much this evening." Velvet responded, "I am listening tonight." Most of the night, she watched me. Our hosts noticed that also.

It was getting late. The Barksdales would have probably stayed up all night reading and talking. You could see they were used to this kind of thing.

They thanked Velvet for bringing me along, and told me to look them up the next time I was in town. I agreed and we left. Velvet told me that the Barksdales used to be hippies. "They actually showed me some pictures of them in San Francisco in the 60s." "That's a leap from then to now," was my reaction. Velvet gave me the car keys and said, "I knew you would enjoy their company." "The night's not over yet." "Hear, hear!"

She tapped her hand on the dashboard. She then dug her nails into my arm. I did not move.

The Substitute

Chapter Eight

What a Difference a Day Makes

The Substitute

The next day brought events that would be life-altering for me. When I got out of bed that morning, I changed into my sweats and went down to the exercise area. Velvet had George install a pro-style gym with bikes, treadmills, weights and other resistance type machines. It had become a routine for me to work out a couple of hours. That's when Velvet would be away on her daily business. George was just finishing his workout. I asked him if he left anything down there for me to lift.

George was a great guy. "Amir, you should have been a linebacker!" "Bad knees, George." He wished me a good workout. I was in the gym for two hours. Velvet appeared in the doorway with a big smile on her face. "I am pregnant! I am pregnant!" She ran across the room, jumped into my arms and hugged me, sweat and all. "This is the happiest day of my life! This is what every woman wants – motherhood makes her whole. Thank you, baby! Thank you! Thank you!" She then ran upstairs and got on the phone.

I remember asking myself, 'what now?' My instincts kept trying to tell me something. I wasn't sure what it was, but I knew I was very much in love with this woman and I was going to go with that. When she ran up the stairs, I shouted, "be careful!" She didn't respond. She was too excited. When I went up, she was just finishing up a call. She told me, she had been calling her father and brother and friends to share the news.

I thought this was a good time to ask her about her divorce. The attorney was pressing to get on the docket, and she felt good about him doing that. She was very busy over the next few days; lawyers, the doctor. She told me that the doctor wanted to see me and talk about my overall health and family medical history. I knew she was very particular. I agreed.

I sat in the doctor's office with her. He had a lot of questions for me. He asked me how much I weighed and about my height. I told him I weighed 230 pounds and was

6'3". He explained to me the importance of knowing these things in advance to better predict potential problems for "Mrs. Andrews and the child." This was the first time I heard her last name. "It's alright. Please, continue. I understand."

My prior training started to weigh in. Was my intellect being befogged because of my affections for this beautiful lady? Could this be a hangover from my past life? Again, I smiled inside, thinking 'there is no enemy here. I'm not in danger.' I was retired and in the oil business, living back in America. In all my travels, I had never met anyone like her. So, I was going to roll with it.

The doctor's voice took me back to the present. I looked at her on and off during my entire exchange with him. She smiled and cried. I gave her a tissue from the doctor's desk. She would touch me at times. She was magical and there was nothing I could do to resist her. I didn't even try.

The whole time we were in the doctor's office, her phone was jumping off the hook. I could see the light coming on. She had put it on silent, but you could still hear it vibrate. We returned to the car. She was quiet at first. Then she said, "I love you, Amir." It sounded ominous, but at the same time, I liked hearing it.

I was uneasy. I should have been happy. There was something I couldn't put my finger on. That night, she was extremely affectionate. All my anxiety was gone by morning. I almost felt embarrassed for having any apprehensions the day before.

I was happy to be with her. The next day, I was a little down because I had to leave that night. There was so much more we needed to talk about. She tried to cover a lot of ground. She reminded me to talk to my boss about relocating here. She talked about naming the baby and her pending divorce. She talked more than I remember her ever talking. It was almost like a nervous kind of a talk. I figured it was because she was going through the pregnancy thing.

She told me she wanted to visit New York to see where I lived and where I worked and played. I asked her when she wanted to come for a visit. She was going to do that after she put to rest some pressing business matters here. "In two weeks, everything should be done here." "Good! That's when we will schedule your visit to New York."

When I left for my flight, it was 9:00 p.m. It was a short flight to New York – less than the usual two plus hours. It was a little after 11:45 p.m. when I arrived in my apartment. There was still something in the air that I couldn't put my finger on. An hour later, she called to find out if I was home. It seemed that every time I heard her voice, my concerns were eased. She told me she missed me already.

I needed some help sleeping that night. Chamomile tea wasn't going to do it. After being barraged with a thousand thoughts, I finally fell asleep. Early the next day, Velvet called and asked if I was able to sleep. She had not slept well at all. She had to go to L. A. to buy a new company to expand her business. She would be gone for at least three days to a week. It all depended on the paperwork and how the transaction went.

The Substitute

Chapter Nine

Played!

The Substitute

A week had passed, and I heard nothing from her. I gave it a few more days. 'This is unusual', I thought. I didn't have any other number to call – just the one she had given me. I was worried. She could have been kidnapped. She was a rich woman. She could have been in a set-up. She could have been in an accident. Four more days passed, and I heard nothing. That Friday morning, I caught a flight.

When my plane landed, I took a cab to her house. When I got there, a "For Sale" sign was in the front yard, and the grass had not been cut. The gate was open. I told the taxi driver to wait. I gave him a hundred-dollar bill; he turned the engine off and waited. I looked around the property. It was deserted. No George, no dogs, no Sarah. Nothing.

By then, my heart was racing. I was grabbing for straws or anything that made sense. I went back to the taxi. I asked the driver if he knew where "The Capital" was located. He said that isn't the name anymore. "What do you mean?" I asked.

"That was the name two weeks ago. Not anymore, mister. It's one of them foreign spots where they have strange food, and they smoke water pipes. I took some people there yesterday."

"Take me there!"

"You bet."

We arrived at the location. It was exactly as he told me. I asked him to wait again and gave him a fifty-dollar bill. He turned the engine off. I wanted to be sure about everything before I decided a course of action. I went inside. The hostess wanted to seat me. I told her that I just wanted to see the new place. I asked if she knew what happened to the prior ownership. They had sold the business, and as far as she knew, the previous owners had moved out of town. The place was completely different. I thanked her and left.

As I walked back towards the taxi, a small statured man came out of the side door of the building. "Hey, Mr.!

Hey, Mr.!" "Yes, what is it?" He told me that he used to work there when it was called "The Capital".

"I was the bus boy back then. I remember, you came in there a few times. I remember you, because Ms. Velvet never talked to the customers like she talked to you and she never spent any time with them either. The staff all wondered about this guy, meaning you, of course. Then one day, it came to me. You look like her husband John."

"Are you serious, man?"

"I'll could be kin to one another."

Things were starting to fall in place now. I had one more thing to do before I made a phone call. The cabbie was playing his CD player. I got into the taxi. He turned the music off and asked, "Where to, mister?'

Chapter Ten

A Man Scorned

The Substitute

"You okay, mister?" the cabbie asked.
"I'm fine. Main and Riverside," I instructed quickly.

When we approached the street, I could see that it as well was no longer the place it had been before. I asked the driver to take me to the airport. What the hell was going on? I had had enough. Then it all became obvious. I was used for something. A patsy. I don't think there was ever a divorce filed at all. There was the hesitation in giving her full name. This guy couldn't get her pregnant. But why me? I was a damn sperm donor! If only I could get my hands on both of them. Who knows if there are two of them?

I was getting angrier with every minute. I had to stop and think. This shit must have been planned all along. Though there were some pieces missing, I had ignored all my instincts, all my training. The signs were there all along. I had disregarded them because I was in love with the woman. Gloves off now, buddy!

Despite all my rage, I had to give her credit. She played it to the max. In a different circumstance, I would have given her a "high five." I needed time to think. We arrived at the airport. The driver said, "You don't owe me anything, mister. You have a safe flight." I thanked him and exited the taxi. It was a two hour-flight to New York. As soon as I entered the apartment, I took a lavender shower. I stayed in there for at least half an hour. I put on some Reiki healing music. I had to relax. This time chamomile tea worked. I needed to relax, not sleep. Sleep would come naturally after I chilled. When I awoke in the morning, I was thinking clearly again. I called the dealership. It was a place I would call when I had a car trouble.

"May I speak to Terry?"
"Who is calling?"
"David Chan."

"Hold on, I'll see if he is here." He muffled the phone. "Hey Terry, there's a guy on the phone who wants to talk to you."

"Who is it?"

"David Chan."

"Wait a second." It took Terry a few minutes to come to the phone. As I think now, he probably knew who it was all the time and expected the call.

"Amir, where the hell are you? What's going on?"

"We need to talk, Terry."

"You okay?"

"Not really."

Terry had a roofing job and he would see me there at nine a.m. An hour later, we met. "Amir, you sounded pissed, my man," he remarked. "Somebody set me up, Terry. This shit was too sophisticated for a civilian." Terry asked me what happened. I went over the whole story with him from start to finish.

"Seriously? Look Amir, you are a true friend. You saved my life. Let me see if any of our people were involved. I'll tell you what I can, if there is anything to tell. You know how this works."

"Sure, whatever you can do, T. I'd appreciate it."

"I'll make some calls. This will be for your information only. You have to assure me, Amir that you won't take any action if it's something you don't like."

"You have my word," I promised.

"I know how you feel. How many times have you done the same thing, man? We called you the 'Casanova' of the agency."

"Yeah, I know. It will help me just to know. I'll meet you at the garage tomorrow the same time. Thanks, Terry."

I slept well that night. Tomorrow, I would have some indication of what happened and why. Finally.

Chapter Eleven

Licking Your Wounds

The Substitute

I wanted all this behind me as soon as possible. I was going to meet Terry at 4 p.m. the next day. I hoped that meeting would shed some light on this incident. Otherwise, it would just be left to my imagination.

I was at the Lynch Marina 4 p.m. sharp. Terry was on the boat waving me aboard. As I remember thinking at the time, Ms. Anderson, a.k.a. Velvet, and her husband John were together in Niger at that very moment. There were no divorce papers filed, no animosity and no separation. None of it was true.

Terry and I set out on the Hudson. He started by saying, "When you left the agency, we were just getting more involved in sub-Saharan Africa. There was Intel to suggest that different groups were setting up camp. We were going to be there too. We saw this guy." I interrupted, "JOHN ANDREWS!"

"RIGHT!" he replied, "Yes. He was pretty well-placed. He knew the groups who were dissatisfied as well as the government people who were corrupt. He knew his way around over there. He was the person we needed at the time. It took a while to convince him. He finally came on board."

"For how long?"

"I can't remember. We get strange requests from time to time. You know that. You've been there. This guy couldn't have kids. He wanted us to find someone who looked like him. We found 67 matches. We asked him to choose. I think you can fill in the blanks. The boss was very happy. I remember him saying, 'One of our own'!"

"That shit ain't funny, Terry." I thought, 'the coincidence and irony of it all'. Terry stated that the guy wanted a donor. "You got to be kidding me!" I reacted. "I kid you not my friend," he reassured me.

"We could see you were falling pretty hard for this lady. We felt it was time to put a move on this and pull the plug. You know Amir, you were a rising star at the agency. Have you ever thought about coming back?"

"I think about it sometimes. I also thought about the many close calls. I liked the rush; but I started to feel I was losing my edge, especially after the shoot-out in Chile. I almost bought the farm."

"But you saved my life!" Terry shouted.

"You would have done the same, Terry."

Laying back against the seat, he continued: "You will know as much as I can tell you, and what I can tell you is all I know. My suggestion is to walk away, Amir. You never know how these things turn out." We were heading back to the marina. I thanked Terry and told him, "I'm done with it."

In the meantime, Velvet was being questioned by her husband about the donor. He wanted to know if she met him. She told him "no." It was a simple procedure. That was it. That seemed to make him feel better about the whole thing. He would never know how much I loved her. Nor would he know the depth of our attachment; or the deception that I was subjected to and how I was played like a piano. She had delivered! He would now have a son to leave his fortune to.

The agency spoke with my boss, Jack, and made arrangements for me to take a leave of absence. That was the least they could do after the bullshit they had put me through. I guess that was their own way of saying 'you are still okay.'

I left for Trinidad. I stayed there for a year and half. When I returned to New York, I was assigned to a new office in Paris. I lived there for 4 years. Every now and then, I would think of Velvet and my son or daughter; I didn't really want to know which. I had walked away as I promised Terry. When I met other women, I kept comparing them to Velvet – she was unique.

I never asked about her again.

Chapter Twelve

Instant Family

The Substitute

Ten years had gone by since that trauma. I had begun to write again. I was involved with a workshop, poetry, etc. I relocated to upstate New York.

One day, I walked down to the local coffee shop where they served Jamaican Blue Mountain coffee. Sometimes I would just sit there, read the paper and write. It was a good environment for some of the things I liked doing, and as far removed as possible from noise.

A had a cup or two of the Jamaican blend, when the owner turned up the volume on the TV. There was a news flash across the screen. After a civil unrest in Niger, several dozen people had been killed, including some Americans. I got up from the table, went outside, and called the dealership. Terry answered. "I knew you would be calling. I'll call you later." I knew how that worked. It could have been 15, 8 or even zero minutes to wait.

There were different reports coming from the media. I would have to wait until I heard back from Terry. At that moment, everything came rushing back – all the events of a decade ago. Everything came back with a vengeance! I was hyped. Five hours later, my phone rang. "A is done! B and C are ok." Click! That was all. That was it. If I didn't get it, too bad. I got it! I knew somebody had exposed her husband. He was probably killed first. I was still in love with her. I wanted to be with her right then. But I knew better than to hope; that never worked. With these situations, it either was or it wasn't. It was just that simple. I had to gather myself all over again.

Six months had gone by. I heard nothing. The Niger story wasn't front page anymore.

As I remember, it was a Saturday evening in the fall of that year. Terry was calling me, asking me to open the door. He was out front. I saw a car parked on the grass. It was Terry's. I was glad he was coming over. I was hoping to get some insight into the situation.

I opened the door; it was Velvet and my daughter – there was no doubt. Velvet asked, "Could we come in?" A million thoughts rushed through my head. I said, "Of course!"

Terry waited until the door closed before he drove away with fall leaves trailing his car.

Epilogue

About the Author

C. E. Shy has been writing since the seventh grade. He continued writing through high school, until he became more involved in sports. After his graduation, he worked at the White Motors Company where he wrote for the company's newspaper. He started a column called: "The Poet's Corner." That was his first published work.

With a one-way ticket, he moved to Sweden. He met a Swedish photographer and started writing narratives for some of the photographs which were sold to newspapers and magazines.

After returning to the US, he joined a poetry workshop that was run by Russell Atkins and Norman Jordan from 1966 to 1968. He stopped writing for years, then started to write again in the late 90s, crafting novellas, flash fiction and poetry. He joined a writing workshop in Cleveland, Ohio in 2011 to hone his writing skills.

Other Books

and

Other Works

by the Author

C. E. Shy

M. A. Shaheed

Celebrating 50: The Legacy of the Muntu poets of Cleveland by K (February 18, 2018) ~ Poetic Prose

"The Pot!": Poetic Reflections of the Glenville Riots 1968 Cleveland, Ohio (February 18, 2018) ~ Poetry

Mixed Emotions (January 3, 2017) ~ Poetry

Five Minutes Past Midnight (January 29, 2017) ~ Novel

Pens and Needles (January 29, 2017) ~ Poetry

Mr. Gentleman. Nomenclature (February 2, 2017) ~ Audio CD

Sketchings (February 19, 2017) ~ Poetry

PTSD Poems That Say Dream (March 14, 2017)

Traveling in the Light (March 21, 2017) ~ Poetry

Transparent-S (April 24, 2017) ~ Poetry

Tuned In (April 24, 2017) ~ Poetry

More Questions Than Answers (June 1, 2017) ~ Poetry

Gray Area (June 1, 2017) ~ Poetry

Balance (June 27, 2017) ~ Poetry

If I Only Could . . . (August 1, 2017) ~ Poetry

Zero at the End of the Rainbow (August 31, 2017) ~ Poetry

Miles to Go While I Weep (September 26, 2017) ~ Poetry

Signs and Signals (October 7, 2017) ~ Poetry

Watch Out (October 24, 2017) ~ Poetry

A Knock on the Door (October 24, 2017) ~ Poetry

Chapter Z (October 29, 2017) ~ Poetry

The Muntu Poets of Cleveland by Russell Atkins (January 8, 2016) ~ Anthology

The Long and the Short of it: Armchair Chronicles. Volume I, II and III (January 28, 2016) ~ A Short Story Collection

The House (January 28, 2016) ~ Novel

Me and Maysun (February 28, 2016) ~ A Collection of Literary Works

Approaching the Ninth Dimension (April 10, 2016) ~ Poetic Prose

Deliver Me from Unconsciousness (June 7, 2016) ~ Poetic Prose

The Visit (June 12, 2016) ~ Novel

The Door at the End of the Hall (August 22, 2016) ~ Poetry

Point Blank! Eclections 4 (September 19, 2016) ~ Poetry

No U Turns ONE WAY! (October 4, 2016) ~ Poetic Prose

The Glimpse: A Remote View (November 7, 2016) ~ Poetry

Cyber Man (November 9, 2016) ~ Novel

A Frayed (December 11, 2016) ~ Poetry

Straight Up! Compilation 1 (December 30, 2016) ~ A collection of poems written by the original members of the Muntu Poets of Cleveland with musical accompaniment

Ain't No Change! Compilation 2 (December 30, 2016) ~ A collection of poems written by the original members of the Muntu Poets of Cleveland with musical accompaniment

Time Share (March 20, 2015) ~ Novel

Substitutions (March 20 2015) ~ Novel

Eclections 2: Words in the Wind (March 20, 2015) ~ Poetry and Prose

Eclections 3. Words in My Window (April 27, 2015) ~ Poetry and Prose

Powhims and Proz   October 30, 2015 Poetry and Prose

Inner Child Press

Inner Child Press is a publishing company founded and operated by writers. Our personal publishing experiences provide us an intimate understanding of the sometimes-daunting challenges writers, new and seasoned may face in the business of publishing and marketing their creative "Written Work".

For more information:

Inner Child Press

<u>www.innerchildpress.com</u>

<u>intouch@innerchildpress.com</u>

Inner Child Press International

'building bridges of cultural understanding'

202 Wiltree Court, State College, Pennsylvania 16801

74

www.ingramcontent.com/pod-product-compliance
Lightning Source LLC
Chambersburg PA
CBHW030150200626
46812CB00016B/1771